THE TRAPDOOR

THE TRAPDOOR

Short story

M.I.A

English translation from the original French
by John H. Temple

ISBN: 978-2-37011-194-4
Éditions Hélène Jacob – 13 Impasse Victor Gesta – 31200
Toulouse – France
Printed by Create Space – USA
9.45 €
Registration of copyright: July 2014

The trapdoor is perfectly smooth.

Now I understand why they asked me to take off my shoes. Socks slip easily on this kind of brushed metal surface, probably too easily. When the time comes, nothing will happen to spoil my fall, giving everyone a nice show.

But with another seven minutes before the scheduled time, I'm trying to stay focused on my feet, which have a tendency to spread away from each other. Stress, no doubt, makes me sweat and dampens my socks somewhat, which is terribly annoying.

Because it would be the last straw if I collapsed before the time comes. It would screw up whatever protocol they seem so sensitive about maintaining. Just so the Guardian doesn't bother me, I'm trying to keep my feet in position behind the red line and not move in the slightest.

My left sock has a hole on top, near my big toe. I should have thought about that kind of thing before leaving my cell and asked for another pair. After all, even when in my situation, one has the right to maintain one's dignity. Now it's too late and it's going to annoy me right up til the end. It would be useless talking to the man standing behind me, he won't answer me. As soon as someone is standing on the trapdoor, nobody can speak to them, except for that final ritual question.

Seven minutes, soon six. The wall clock conscientiously does its job. You might think that standing without batting an eyelid for a handful of additional seconds would not be too complicated… well, if that's what you think, I'll invite you to come and take my place.

Because the problem with the trapdoor isn't only that it might eventually open… it's that I've already been here for almost an hour with a rope around my neck…

1 – THE BANK

Everything went wrong starting with the bank robbery. Five weeks of preparation only to lose three members in less than an hour, I'd call that a fiasco, even if Ricky insisted upon simply referring to events as "problems".

Ricky was a moron. Twenty years old, putting on airs of being a hard-ass, which fooled nobody, and an unconvincing tendency to want to play the "real professional". The "problem", as he'd probably have liked to say himself, is that Ricky is no longer here to talk about it, since he's dead. Not at the bank, but a few days later, when we tried to retrieve the others who had been separated from us during the robbery and when the fiasco then turned into a total disaster.

No, that's a bunch of crap… Ricky got it during the van episode; it was Orson who went before him. Now I'm getting all mixed up… I thought I could stay calm until the end, but the trapdoor is having the same effect on me as it would on anyone else in my position. I am right on the brink of pissing my pants.

If I can manage to get my thoughts in order, that will help me hold on until the end. Perhaps that will also stop me from watching the clock which seems to be making fun of me. I simply need to remain focused and review things right from the beginning.

For the bank job, there were eight of us, including two girls who had no business being there, if you want my opinion. Lana, a fiery brunette with a hard look in her eyes, her only criminal experience being to take off with a cash register and get snagged, and Sally, a little blond angel with a round belly, who hadn't paid her rent for ages and picked through the trash to eat. Sally was pregnant. It shows you how one hundred million can motivate the unlikeliest of robbers. They are both dead too now.

I am the last to go.

The general organization of the robbery was entrusted to Karl, a guy I took an immediate dislike to but who subsequently, I must admit, knew exactly what he wanted. Let's say that out of all of us, he was the least incompetent to put together a viable plan. The kind of guy who'd rip off his classmates starting back in primary school by reselling them the marbles he had just stolen from them. I also think that he was the biggest bastard of the bunch, even counting Lucas, who was a hell of a scumbag. The proof is that Karl managed to last a little longer... but then not as long as me, which leads me to wonder: was I not, ultimately, the worst of them all?

What is certain, is that I kind of liked old man Orson, a wrinkled bearded man who looked like he'd come back from absolutely everything, including his own life. He and I had very nice long and silent conversations. I've never managed to know anything about what he was doing before we found ourselves all bogged down in this quagmire. I don't think any of that is of much importance now. There is just me left here with that damn hole in my sock making me feel horribly ashamed.

Shit, there I go again...

The bank we chose, out of the eight WSB branch offices in the city, was in a small gray building, where its outside ugliness did not reflect at all what it had within its walls. We could have found a more prestigious one, but it was supposed to have the least sophisticated security system. In fact, we essentially trusted Karl about this, because none of us really had any idea what we were doing.

Afterwards, I was asked why I had gotten involved in such a scheme, as my only real skill was in stealing cars and even that was something I was rusty at doing. What do you want me to say? The idea had just seemed good at the time, as it must have for the others. It's a little like asking a neurosurgeon why they would improvise as a cardiologist in a moment of despair. There is always a reason that makes us take the plunge, even if one can't really identify what it is. But I admit I had no idea how things would turn out. I especially didn't have an inkling of just how bad I'd be with a gun.

The weapons were only supposed to intimidate the faint-hearted, that's all. We had not expected that they would be used and only Tony and Orson really seemed to know what they were doing with them. Tony had been a champion shot in his hometown and Orson had possibly taken part in the last war, for all I know. Karl was good at throwing knives. He did tricks to impress the girls, at first. The sort of guy who says "I can hit an apple blindfolded from 10 meters away". A bastard and in addition a show-off...

Lucas was just good for hitting people and he loved crushing Ricky's fingers whenever he had a chance, just to remind him which of the two was the real tough guy. It should be said that Ricky's experience as a criminal only officially amounted to a single count of arson. Compared to the fourteen guys the other one had laid out in a bar one evening in a brawl, he didn't weigh out as being much of a heavy. But I've always had the secret hope that Lucas would wake up one night with his ass on fire. Unfortunately I never had that pleasure.

All that just to say that concerning our handling of guns, we were screwed. Fortunately, Lana was damn good at batting her eyelashes when it became necessary, and Sally was a good actress. Karl therefore decided to come up with, and I quote, a "psychological" rather than an "aggressive" type plan. When I think about the end result, I wonder if it wouldn't have been better to have chosen the second option.

Behind me, I can hear the quiet breathing of the Guardian. I had almost forgotten the guy because he's been so quiet. In what has been nearly an hour, he hasn't even so much as cleared his throat once. He takes his job so seriously that I feel almost as much pity for him as I do for myself. Well I may be exaggerating a bit there...

To come back to the plan, Karl's idea was simple enough: a driver would wait for the others out on the street, five people would go into the bank and two others would deal with making the outside telephone call. Obviously, everyone began to vie for the comfortable spot in the van, which shows you how much we wanted to go in there. Lucas ended up clouting Tony, who was the most stirred up, so that he would stop and listen to what Karl had to propose. That whack sounded out so loud that the issue was resolved in record time.

From that point on the roles were distributed quickly: the two girls, Orson, Tony and myself would go into the bank. Lucas was to accompany Karl – they went well together, those two – for the phone call. Ricky would remain outside and would be our driver. I believe that his unpredictable pyromaniac side scared the daylights out of Karl, who did not want his plan to fail due to a trash fire. And then he must have thought that I might possibly be more convincing with a gun, when he had to choose between Ricky and me to be the fifth man. But as for determining a choice he could have just as well flipped a coin, considering how badly I managed.

But hey, I wanted to save my teeth and therefore didn't want to annoy that colossus Lucas, when Karl assigned me that role. And plus it didn't seem all that complicated, at least not on paper. I was only supposed to look nasty, watching over the bank customers as if I were the type of guy who shaves with a machete, and most especially I was not to talk to anyone, in order to remain believable. Karl told me several times that I had a tendency of being way too nice. I would guess that coming out of his mouth, this was not a compliment.

Orson and Tony, the pros with the guns, were to provide a bit of realism to the situation by waving their weapons around in a convincing way toward any of those who refused to cooperate. I must admit that they played their role well and that I might even have taken them for being genuine traditional type bank robbers. For my part, I believe that I managed coming across as not being too ridiculous. Well... at least until things started to go out of control.

At 2 pm, we went into the bank. We had chosen Monday, because Karl had spent several weeks verifying the bank director's routine. On Monday afternoons, he was always absent. And Karl wanted it to be the assistant director who would deal with Lana, because he had children. The director was single and so therefore did not fit the plan. We needed a weak link.

So anyway, at 2 pm., we were all in place, among a dozen customers. The girls came in exactly one minute before the other three of us. Lana, with a plunging neckline and tears in her eyes, asked the teller to call the director for a matter of utmost importance. While Lana was performing her bit, Sally was pretending to consult the pamphlets on display in the middle of the lobby, in order to also appear busy. Tony stood at an ATM, as if to consult his account, while Orson simulated a telephone conversation in a low voice and I... I confess that I do not really remember how I tried to pull the wool over people's eyes. Luckily we didn't have to wait too long, because I'm sure I must have looked suspicious.

When the assistant director finally appeared behind the counter to talk with Lana, Sally dropped her brochure and became very pale, hands pressed against her clearly rounded belly. I'm not sure how she managed, but her fake dizzy spell certainly caused a stir. She collapsed in a heap on the ground and the only security guard present – who seemed terribly bored – quickly went over to her to see what was wrong.

While he was leaning over her and was trying to pick her up without touching her big belly, Orson approached from behind and discreetly tasered him with an electrical jolt to his lower back. He had been the one who convinced Karl of the need to limit any physical injuries and had managed to prevail on this particular point. So the security guard was there on the floor without having any time to squeal. Meanwhile, Tony had left the ATM and had taken out his weapon, just as I had. People's screams began to be heard when Sally herself jumped up, helped by Orson, and took out a miniature pistol from her purse.

From a distance, I saw Lana hold out her phone to the assistant director, who in turn rapidly became very pale. Karl and Lucas were both right on schedule. On the other end of the line, the wife and children of the poor guy must have been trying to explain to him that there were two violent men, one of whom was missing half of his teeth, who were in his living room a few kilometers away. I did not hear what was said but the method appeared to be convincing, because he returned the device to Lana without saying anything and immediately began to use his touch screen. While she dictated some numbers to him, I could see his fingers going like crazy and he did not give the impression that he was trying to delay anything.

Up until that point, everything was going well. Karl had told us that the element of surprise would play in our favor. I should say, if I'm not mistaken, that this was the first bank robbery anywhere in over fifteen years. The previous one had dated to before the implementation of the comprehensive reform of the penal system. At a time when you could still pilfer an apple from a fruit stand without getting six months. Today, you would be crazy to steal anything from a grocer and I won't even mention the banks. Crazy or completely desperate, as was our case.

The advantage for those who do have the stomach for it is that security has become a joke. Something that is just there for decoration really, a reminder of days gone by, nothing more. The government relies solely on the concept of dissuasion and it works perfectly. Theft has become an exception because repression is handled so ruthlessly. Who would take the risk of being sent directly to prison to rot behind bars for the rest of their life?

In the previous century, it seems that the law worked on the basis of something they called the presumption of innocence. A trial could take years and the accused would have rights. Today however, sanctions are immediately applied, thanks to the efficiency of the Module, which centralizes all data. Someone who steals on Monday and is busted on Tuesday is in prison on Wednesday, and that will be for at least six months, but more often than not it will be for twenty years. Simple, fast and effective. Unless one manages not to get caught.

Those who do try are fewer and fewer and make do with committing minor crimes that have limited impact. Nobody is crazy enough to even imagine going after one hundred million urkans. We were the only lunatics in the world to even consider the idea, not to mention actually taking the plunge. And today? I am the only one left, standing here on top of the trapdoor.

When I say that everything went well, I mean concerning the bank transfer. Lana obtained our millions in less than three minutes, so we cannot blame her. But Tony wanted to play the tough guy for the security cameras, rather than watching the people behind the counter. I did not exactly see what happened, but one of the tellers must have pressed the right button before Orson had time to move everybody out into the lobby. The result is that the local cops arrived two minutes too soon.

We needed those two minutes to leave the bank, climb into the van and take off. That idiot Tony, wanting to show off and taunt the security system rather than do his job, deprived us of that critical head start. While going out the door, we heard shouts and warning shots, and understood things were not going to end well, especially as Sally couldn't run very fast. After that… I don't remember everything.

Orson yelled at Tony not to play the hero, but to take off and join Ricky who was quietly waiting behind the wheel. Lana sprinted across the road and I remember thinking that robbers in the old days must have been really courageous. Because if we had had to do the same thing while carrying bags full of money, nobody would have ever managed to reach the vehicle. Inevitably, Tony didn't listen to anyone and stopped in the middle of the street shouting "I'll cover you!" With just a simple pistol against Impulse lasers, he didn't manage to cover very much. He was sliced up in no time, while Orson pulled Sally along by the hand to hurry her up.

As for me, when I saw pieces of Tony lying on the ground, I lost my head and started shooting in the direction of the cops while continuing to run, even while Ricky was driving away. I think I hit two shop windows, a car and a big garbage dumpster. In the panic, I also nearly shot myself in the foot. But my shots missed the police by several meters, who quickly understood that I was just a dumb amateur, so oddly enough they spared me. Fortunately, Orson and Sally were moving behind me so at least I didn't hit them. But they were far too slow and Ricky did not want to wait.

I only had time to throw myself through the side door, where Lana was reaching for me, while the van took off with smoking tires. Turning my head, I saw Orson behind me who watched us leaving, while Sally threw herself on her knees with her hands in the air to escape being cut down by the lasers. I think the old man saw on my face just how sorry I was, but maybe I'm imagining things.

The cops did not even try to follow us. They must have relied on having Orson and Sally to quickly spill the beans about us. Lana therefore had the good idea to call Karl and Lucas to explain the situation and ask them to change their hideout. From what I could hear, Karl was incredibly angry and wasn't trying to hide it. But he eventually confirmed the alternative address by screaming it out, before hanging up on her.

When we got there thirty minutes later, there were only five of us left and we had a huge problem on our hands. If they broke down and said anything, Orson and Sally would begin by giving the main hideout, as we had agreed. But eventually they would also give some of the other addresses, once the cops returned empty-handed and upset. It was only a matter of time. We spent a bitch of an evening considering a number of possibilities. The solution that we finally chose was probably poorly implemented, because the next day, we added two more deaths to the tally.

There are only five minutes left now on the clock.

I have the beginning of a cramp in my right calf. The more I try to relax the more it becomes painful. It's hot in this room and I'm thirsty. I'm thirsty, in pain and I'm ashamed of that fucking hole in my sock.

But more than anything else, I'm afraid.

2 – THE POLICE STATION

Karl, Lucas, Lana, Ricky and me. Things appeared really pitiful to us when we reviewed our undertaking. One death and two others caught, that wasn't a very good average for a start.

Tony had been directly responsible for the fiasco, but Karl considered everyone to be a bunch of amateurs, without distinction, and sputtered copiously over Ricky, even though he had been the only one not to have set foot in the bank. Behind him, Lucas cracked his knuckles unpleasantly and the sound got on my nerves.

I wanted a shower and an anti-migraine patch, but in that particular backup hideout, the facilities were not very good and we had no hot water. As for the patch, it wasn't going to happen…

After having balled us out completely, Karl seemed to feel better. He ended up calming himself down a bit by playing with his knife. Lana took advantage of his being calmer to ask a question that had also been running around in my head for quite a while. What were we going to do about the others?

Lucas made a weird face, Ricky stopped fiddling with the bracelet around his right wrist and Karl threw his knife slightly harder than usual. The blade quivered a few seconds in the back wall. The question did not seem to please them and there was an uncomfortable moment of silence in the room. In a spirit of chivalry toward Lana, or by pure desire to piss off Karl – I confess that I am not sure which of the two motivated me – I repeated the question after her. So yes, what about the others, what were we going to do for them?

Karl looked at me with a disgusted expression. Rather more than my sweaty smell, I think that my so-called nice-guy character was bothering him. Or what surely in his eyes was my weakness of character.

He answered with the tone of someone dealing with an intellectually challenged individual to say that the others would just have to fend for themselves without us. I seem to remember that he added that losing an old man and a knocked-up girl was not the worst that could have happened to us. As far as finding alternative hideouts, he knew where we could go. A place that only he knew about and that the cops could not discover thanks to our colleagues, even if they did become too talkative.

Lana called Karl a big rotten cowardly bastard. Just enough to trigger an urge in Lucas to hit someone, who looked at her with a nasty expression before saying that he could not bear having hysterical women around. Sprawling in an armchair that stank of dust and piss, Ricky sank down, as if the threat of being slapped around was directed toward him. A nervous tic started up in my left eye but I kept my cool and decided to just stay calm. Though the image I couldn't get out of my mind with Tony being sliced to pieces in the middle of the street did not really help me.

But from what I had just heard, curiously I was the only one to remember an essential element, a detail that would stop any discussion and shut Karl's trap. An unstoppable argument.

Orson knew the access code. It was as simple as that. Without Orson, no code and with no code, no money. Even if Lana had the number of the account that the money had been transferred to, Orson was the only one to be able to get access to it.

We had chosen two names at random the first night, when

we had to decide who would be responsible for each one of the main elements of our organization. The addresses of the hideouts were only known to Karl. I for one had been glad it was a woman along with the most normal guy of the group who would be in possession of the information involving the money. The principle was simple: by avoiding a situation where everyone would be aware of everything, we also avoided the possibility that one of the more vicious among us might suddenly want to get rid of their partners earlier than necessary.

Anyway, Lana had chosen the account number and Orson had the access code. Without Orson, we were simply five idiots just as poor as before, but with a thousand more problems.

That is pretty much what I said during my modest statement to them, taking a perverse pleasure in seeing Karl suddenly remember and explode with a volley of expletives. Lucas merely groaned but that was better than nothing. Lana gave me a knowing wink and I suddenly felt much more sure of myself. But that did not last long.

Karl quickly regained control of himself and of the operations. If we had to retrieve Orson and "the blonde", as he called her, we shouldn't lose any time and had to manage a night operation. According to him, the police station, which was already a quiet place during the day, was nearly deserted at night. Inevitably, the staff was limited as there were nearly no criminals to manage. People who were arrested never stayed for more than twelve hours in these neighborhood stations, before being shipped off to the nearest Center, whether they were locked up for a few days or for the remainder of their lives. Karl said we might expect to come across two cops on duty, three at the most.

For the first time since our arrival, Ricky spoke up. He knew the place, because that was where he had ended up the day he was brought in for arson. He added that it was only a few years ago, so the place must not have changed much since.

A one-story square building, with a large open area at the front for the public, a section of cells down a hallway on the right and a reserved area for the cops on the left. A cloakroom, showers, weapon lockup, that sort of thing. At the back of the area prohibited to the public, another door opening out onto an alley behind the building. According to Ricky, we could get in through there. All we had to do was to wait until the shift change at 11 pm, when the night cops arrived for work. We just had to hope that this was still their routine.

He scribbled a vague sort of floor plan on a piece of paper that Karl handed him and added a few words in very shaky handwriting. Ricky did not seem to be himself either, and Lucas looked at him mockingly.

Lana walked over to what passed for a sink, to get herself a glass of water. The brown liquid sputtering out of the tap disgusted her so much that she no longer felt thirsty. She returned to slump down in another armchair, the same color as the water. She now seemed more depressed than angry and began staring at her wrist thoughtfully. I wanted to take her in my arms and tell her that everything would turn out alright, but I hate lying to people I care about. So I preferred to shut up and wait to hear what kind of solution Karl was evidently going to come up with.

As it turned out he put together a plan that didn't seem any worse from any other, which involved us leaving from where we were fairly quickly, in order to get there in good time. The changeover to the night shift was not going to wait and if we missed this opportunity, Orson and Sally would definitely be transferred in the morning by the larger day shift. That would mean goodbye code and all those urkans we had managed to get transferred. Therefore we quickly worked out the final details and at 10 pm we left the seedy apartment that had served us as a temporary refuge.

Lucas had the bright idea of bringing along a box of energy bars which we chewed in silence along the way to the police station. Sitting beside him in the front, Ricky started to show signs of nervousness which seemed to bother Karl. Just for doing that, I felt like thanking him. But I preferred to stay quiet and chew on another energy bar, the idea being to keep my mouth shut.

Meanwhile, Karl tried to convince Lana that keeping the account number to herself was no longer a good idea. Not with the risks the group was taking. She stayed silent for a while, and then wrote a sequence of numbers on a small grimy piece of paper which she handed to me, while looking Karl directly in the eyes. He didn't say anything but I saw his hands tense. I pocketed the information and acknowledged it with a simple nod, without saying a word. I didn't think it was the time to trigger a new shouting match which might lead to a fistfight.

When we arrived in the alley behind the police station, it was 10:30 pm. and the place was deserted. The curfew which has been in force over the past thirteen years works rather well in these outlying districts. Anyway, there is no reason to loiter outside in such a place. Streetlights illuminate empty sidewalks, gray walls and depressed cats; that's it. Nothing to do and nothing to see.

All that to say that the alley was as empty as possible, but even so we drove up with our headlights off, before stopping a little way back from the entrance which interested us. All we needed to do was watch our timing while trying not to get into an argument with one another.

Ten minutes before the scheduled time, we saw a car pull up and park about a hundred meters away and as expected, we saw the first night-shift cop get out. He calmly headed toward the entrance, without even a glance in our direction. We were lucky, he was alone. His night-shift co-worker would be showing up soon.

Lana silently left the van and began waving her arms and calling for help as soon as the light from the street lamps were on her, which had the desired effect: the guy looked up, assessed the situation, decided that a young woman in distress deserved his attention and ran over to her without hesitating. I braced myself and hoped that she had guessed correctly how loud to call out so that the cops who were still inside the station would not come out.

Lucas hid in the shadows not far away and waited for the right moment. When Lana collapsed on the ground, raised her hands groaning, the man knelt down, trying to understand what she was saying.

By way of explanation, he got hit over the head with Lucas' bat, making a loud crack that gave me goose bumps. Relieved of his Impulse weapon and his magnetic passkey, the cop ended up laid out behind a vehicle, invisible from the street. Two minutes had barely gone by and now we simply had to wait for his colleague, who would soon turn up.

We repeated the operation with the same success, other than

that Lucas went about hitting they guy two more times to be sure, making me nauseous. I told myself that there wouldn't be much chance that this cop would be getting up very soon, given the condition of his skull. He ended up near his partner and Karl stuck two anti-insomnia patches onto their arms, just in case. Having had the misfortune of trying one out once, I knew that they were going to be in a coma for at least sixteen hours.

Lucas wanted to keep the Impulse weapons, even though he knew like everyone else that they were digitally encoded. Unless you also carried around its owner's hand, such a gun was useless. I wanted to remind him of that little detail, but I felt that he really cared about his trophies, so I preferred to let things ride.

We rushed to the door, because time was running out. The two guys on the afternoon shift would begin to notice the delay and get annoyed. When we inserted the magnetic keycard, the door opened without any problem and as expected we found ourselves in a small hallway leading to the locker room and the coffee-break room.

Despite our efforts to be silent, the abrupt clacking sound of the lock was heard by one of the cops in the main room. Off in the other room, we heard someone joke about being late and overtime, before hearing approaching footsteps.

Lucas held his bat out in front of him, Karl had his hands tightened on his gun and Ricky gnawed his last fingernail with anything left to chew. Lana threw me one of those stunning looks only she knew the secret of and I felt my diaphragm tighten with pleasure. Or maybe that was just my fear manifesting itself.

One of the men must have gotten to the locker room, because his steps were now close by. We went up to the end of the hallway to the door on the left, leaning forward while ridiculously walking on tiptoe. Lucas positioned himself against the door jamb, his bat in the air. Karl and I were stopped just behind him, our guns pointing toward the rectangle of light that was taking shape on the ground, ready to shoot at the first knee that emerged from that area.

The footsteps stopped for a few seconds. The cop must have wondered why the locker room was empty and grumbled something incomprehensible before beginning to move toward where we were, just on the other side of the wall. Lucas did not leave him enough time to get past with more than the tip of his nose before he smashed the top of his skull with a clean direct hit. The guy fell forward and Karl cushioned his fall to limit the noise. For the third time that evening, we pulled a body around to stow it out of the way in a dark corner.

In less than twenty minutes, we had managed to accumulate the equivalent of at least sixty years of imprisonment in a Center, for all of us. Or automatic life sentences, if one of the cops turned out to be a corpse. For the second one, of the two lying out there in the street, I had some serious doubts.

I thought that their colleague might be alerted by the noise. We moved slowly through the locker room, after checking to see if it was empty, then approached the door leading to the main office area, where we heard someone talking. He was on the phone and apologizing for being late. We gave him just enough time to hang up before bursting in, guns and bat out front. Understandably, he immediately put up his hands and without too much difficulty accepted that Karl handcuff him to a desk leg that was invisible from the street, gagged him and gave him a healthy dose of artificial sleep in turn.

Lana and Ricky were already running toward the cell block.

Thirty seconds later, Orson and Sally were both back among us, surprised, happy, but with spaced-out expressions and smiles, which were too forced to be natural. They must have had anti-resistance patches forced on them, so they would speak more easily. That too, I had already experienced.

We started on our way out without wasting any time. Upon reaching the locker room, we were all in a much better mood, despite the tension of the last few hours. Lucas even had the amazing kindness to compliment Sally, who thanked him with a nod. Orson and Lana, arm in arm, walked on ahead. She seemed genuinely pleased to have found the old man.

The sound of the triggered Impulse took too much time to go from my ear to my brain. I did not have time to warn them.

Pros would not have failed to check the toilets upon their arrival. We, however, were so totally out of control we had apparently forgotten to find a cop who had managed to stay hidden. As soon as they crossed the threshold, the laser hit them both. Lana, who had taken the shot full-on directly to her head, died instantly. Orson, being taller, got hit close to his neck and survived barely two minutes, with all his blood gushing out. While he was falling to the ground, Lucas rushed into the room shouting and jumped the cop who had managed to fuck everything up and who was not expecting such an onslaught. To my surprise, the bat was the winner as Lucas took his frustration out on the guy.

While he was earning us an additional life sentence and Sally was crying out hysterically, Ricky tried to silence her, and I knelt down next to Orson. The old man made gestures with his hand asking me to lean in closer.

I stuck my ear against his mouth and listened to what he could tell me in the time he had, before suffocating loudly in his own blood.

I rested his head on the floor as gently as I could when I understood that it was all over. I had the weird thought that I had more blood of his on me than what remained inside him. All of a sudden, I would have given anything for an anti-insomnia patch.

Standing up, with sticky hands and strong taste of bile in my mouth, I did my best not to look at Lana's corpse, for fear of seeing her eyes. On the other hand, I could not avoid those of Karl, who was staring at me with an expression that was both hateful and greedy. He had not taken long in understanding what had happened, and I knew that I was going to begin having problems with him very soon.

I was the new holder of the access code to the account and I would have much rather not have been. The hundred million urkans weighed on my shoulders like twelve tons of well compacted shit.

A little less than four minutes left now. It's crazy all that one can remember in a handful of seconds. That cramp is still there but nausea has almost taken over my fear. Thinking about Lana and the old man just makes me want things to end faster now. I would really like the Guardian to ask his question and let me go on to my destiny.

But before then, I still need to remember the van and Sally. Sally lying down with her hands on her belly, showing her slightly angelic smile.

3 – THE ROAD

And now what?

This question went around among what remained of our group during the better part of the night, so nobody could sleep. The third hideout, which served us now as a safe house, was a real dump and anyway there weren't enough mattresses for everyone. We left Sally curled up lying down in a corner so she could recuperate a little and we tried to lower our voices so as not to disturb her.

When Karl brought up the issue of the account and the code in front of Lucas and Ricky, I did not pretend to be surprised. I had been expecting him to start something since leaving the police station. During the entire trip back in the van, he had stared at me in a disturbing way, almost obscenely. If he believed he would impress me, he was wrong because my sadness had woven into me a kind of inner fury, which was far more powerful than his ferret eyes. The desire to make confetti out of the piece of paper Lana had given me just to make him go crazy almost came over me several times, but the memory of her beautiful corpse held me back. A result like that just to drop everything, what a waste.

Then I laid the paper down in front of them on the small wobbly table that separated us, a gesture that I had wanted to seem negligent, as if the information had no importance. Before Karl had time to speak up I added that the code would follow, but I first wanted to know how things were going to turn out. I asked the questions that we had never taken the time to deal with, probably because we did not really think that this moment would ever come.

And now what?

With at least one dead cop chalked up on our slate, we had

significantly increased the seriousness of the situation and would go down another notch in public opinion. Everyone would gladly denounce us as soon as we tried to go out. Why not just turn ourselves in and beg for clemency? According to me, we had no chance of escaping. Not with the means which the Module had at its disposal.

When Karl began to say something, certainly just to call me a coward, Sally's voice could be heard from the depths of the sofa. I remember only a single word of what she said stayed with me. "Mentalist". Everyone froze. Ricky called her crazy, asking what a Mentalist might have anything to do with things. She stood up awkwardly and walked over to speak with me while ignoring the others.

She told me that things had changed since being in her fourth month of pregnancy. Little by little, she had been feeling like she was immune to the weekly brainwashing sessions done by the Center, that they had not been having any effect on her. She could feel their presence and remembered the sensations from having a session, as if ants were crawling under her skull and moving around and around.

The simple fact that she even had this memory was evidence that she was actually immune. Nobody ever has any kind of memory of having a session with a Mentalist. You know that you've been through and suffered from the session, because every inmate is obligated to, but you would never remember what it feels like physically. That is just part of the process.

Sally added that the effect she experienced had increased the previous month and that even people located near her now benefited from this same protection when they were within 50 meters of her. That's why everyone was relieved when she left the Center. They had been forced to isolate her during every Regional Mentalist's visit so he could do his job properly and the guards had been annoyed dealing with the logistics involved.

I went to sit beside her to take her hand and ask her if she knew what this protection could mean. She looked down and told me that yes, she knew. Lucas looked at her with a mixture of horror and respect in his eyes. Apparently he also understood what this meant and therefore was not as ignorant as I had thought. Karl took out his knife, something which showed that he was trying to figure out how this new information might be put to good use. I also began to contemplate this unexpected information, which might just be able to change everything for us.

To be immune to the Mentalists meant that we could approach them without difficulty, simply by neutralizing their escort. And the Regional Mentalist's escort is generally only made up of two men. Cops or a couple of Center guards, depending on the context. Nothing to do with the High Mentalist's escort, since he is always surrounded by at least ten guards. That's normal because he is the only one having his unique functions, while there are more than five hundred Regional Mentalists around the world. They are important but not essential, since there are several to cover each area.

Twice a week, they travel to Centers and brainwash the convicts in order to make them as meek as sheep. This ends the stress, panic attacks, riots and twisted impulses, which might otherwise have a tendency to come out. Thanks to them, a Center can contain fifty thousand people without any problem, having only a handful of guards to watch over everything. Two weekly sessions are enough to keep the place under control and at the same time ensure that the few lucky ones who are discharged will stay out of trouble for quite a while.

The strangest thing about the Mentalists, is that we know of their existence, we know what they do, and yet we accept their mission without batting an eye. The general population probably feels a sense of security that makes people turn a blind eye, but even those who have suffered through one of their brainwashings do not blame them. Intellectually perhaps, but not on a gut-level. They must introduce some sort of chemical into our blood, a high-octane equivalent of an anti-anger patch with permanent effects.

When Sally related this information, we all understood that this could really help change the odds. Only Ricky needed a bit of time to put things together, but when he eventually understood the importance of the news, he gave a hard kick to the coffee table and yelled out that we could all have our ID files erased.

Karl asked him to quiet down but then added that he was right though, since a Mentalist, even from the first level, also had the ability to telepathically connect to the Module simply by thinking, could then erase our tracks in the system, and also create other identities for us. He could literally make us disappear from the databases and allow us to begin a whole new life. A life full of urkans.

Of course, he would only do so under duress and would immediately get inside our heads if there was the slightest breach. But if Sally was telling the truth, she would be our shield. All that we needed was five minutes alone with him. One minute per person, is all the time needed to completely modify a Module file and create a new existence. A blank slate and the right to wander around in front of surveillance cameras without triggering a red alert. If we could get our hands on a Mentalist, we would become untouchable, even if the cops found us a few minutes later.

That rule, set up ten years ago, vaguely resembles the law from ancient times that said that a particular crime could not be tried twice, even if the accused confessed to having committed the crime after his acquittal. A cleansing performed by a Mentalist, when it is done within the Module, follows the same logic to some degree. It is final and without appeal. It means a new virginity in the eyes of the world. An unhoped-for event, which nobody really dares consider. For us, it was the only way we could escape from this crappy situation.

I cut off Karl during his spiel to ask Sally how she wanted to proceed. It was her idea, after all. She told me that the best way to do it was to intercept the Mentalist's van at the coastal road entrance of the Center during his Sunday visit there. It was a good idea but an uncomfortable one. Nobody likes to be less than five kilometers from a Center.

But anyway, our choices were limited. We couldn't stay here forever just waiting. We couldn't take a walk down the street. We couldn't use our money. Now we could not avoid either the cameras or the eyes of people outside. The Module would find us quickly, because it was programmed to track and find us. So we all agreed. We had to wait for the van, stop it and hope that we would thus find a solution to all of our problems.

Seeing the ocean again scared the daylights out of me and I think I ended up going to sleep that night dreaming that I was drowning in the middle of a pile of seaweed. My only consolation was that all of this had diverted attention from everyone and that I was still the only one who knew the code. For the time being.

The next day, we left once night had fallen. We went in the direction of the nearest Center, located more than three hundred kilometers to the North. The Center that we had all personally been to and that admitted convicts coming from the entire ANW zone. The American Northwest. A lousy set of bad memories.

The truck went slowly and we arrived on-site when dawn broke. The sun rose over a desolate beach with gray water. Before us, the seaway stretched out far in front of us to the island Center in the distance. A road that none of us had wanted to see again.

We positioned ourselves among the rocks surrounding the entrance to the bridge, and kept out of sight. We weren't risking much, the place was deserted. No one ever comes and hangs around the entrance of the roads leading to the Centers without having a very good reason to do so. Only inmates take those routes, usually just one way. And of course, the Mentalists.

While waiting, I thought of when I myself had gone along in that direction. The inner panic I felt. The idea of never being able to step foot on the continent again. The impression that those few minutes in transit lasted for hours. Wanting to throw myself into the middle of the toxic seaweed floating in the water around the Center. The certainty that I was going to die.

Seen from the outside, the seaway is nothing other than a tar strip that goes straight across the water at a few meters above it, supported by large concrete pillars. I would have liked to blow up those pillars and watch everything fall apart. But we weren't there for that.

When the time came, Sally gave me a nod. As agreed, I accompanied her to where the seaway officially began. That was where the asphalt was darker, more recent, less worn by vehicles being driven on it. That was where the Mentalist would arrive in a few minutes.

I helped her to lie down across the road and asked her again if she really wanted to take the risk. She looked at me with a slight smile, as if to encourage me to feel a little carefree. Then she squeezed my arm and told me everything was going to work out fine. The van would stop. She could feel it. Telling me this, she took one of my hands and placed it on her belly button. It was the first time I had ever touched a pregnant woman's stomach. The sensation made me feel like crying.

I reluctantly left her there and quickly returned to hide behind the rocks that separated the old coastal road from the beach. Through a gap in the rocks, I could watch her. Out of this whole experience, that is the image that really affected me the most. Sally lying down with her hands on her belly, showing a slightly angelic smile. Her blond hair, spread out on the pitch black asphalt; the silence and the sickening smell of algae. The absurdity of the world, the general situation and that of myself.

The Mentalists' punctuality is always absolute. It seems as if they are programmed that way. Perhaps they really are actually, as no one really knows how they function. In any case, this one was true to their reputation.

We heard the sound of the van before seeing it. I saw Sally close her eyes and her lips move. Perhaps she was praying in her own way. I closed my eyes in turn because a part of me was persuaded that the vehicle wasn't going to stop, although it was impossible not to see her.

The girl had more guts than all of us put together.

The squealing of the brakes so relieved me I thought I was going to piss in my pants. I turned my head to tell the others to be ready to move. That day, the escort was made up of two wardens. A godsend, for these are less likely to draw their Impulse guns than the cops would be. In the Centers it is rare for the personnel to use their Impulses so they end up being out of practice.

I saw the first get off via the back of the van and approach Sally, who kept her eyes closed and her lips from moving. With the tip of his foot, he touched her body, as if to check for a reaction. I thought it was an ugly and cruel gesture and I would have loved punching him in the nose. But it wasn't the right time for that yet. Not as long as the driver was still out of sight.

We knew it was quite possible that the van might simply go ahead and drive around Sally. It was a risk to take, and in this case we still had the option of a frontal attack, which everybody preferred avoiding. But I was counting on the persuasion provided by her distended belly. I was right.

The warden returned towards the van to call out to his co-worker and ask him to come. The driver got out in turn and came over. They began talking in low voices and seemed upset. We did not give them any time to make a decision and came out from behind the rocks, our guns out. Karl's stock of patches was beginning to seriously diminish but he had enough to provide his usual heavy dose of anti-insomnia. They did not resist, clearly aware that artificial sleep was preferable to the finality of death.

I looked around to check out the situation. Six lampposts within forty meters, along with just as many switchboxes.

The Module had all it needed to satisfy its curiosity.

Lucas carried the guards over behind the rocks, tied them together and came back with the two added trophies. I helped Sally up and hugged her tightly. I think I had been more frightened than she had been. She gently left my arms and moved toward the van, which had its back door still open. She seemed curious and almost impatient. I followed her, the other three staying back a few steps behind me.

The Mentalist whom we had captured was older than those I had seen before. In my opinion, he was at an age where he would soon begin to lose his gift. Like all the others, he had blond hair that was almost white and the pupils of his violet eyes were but thin vertical lines. Empty emotionless eyes, which did not appear to show any fear.

Sally climbed in to sit next to him, without speaking. They just examined each other carefully, as if to assess who the other was. He certainly tried to probe her because he frowned slightly after a few seconds. He then turned toward me.

I understood what Sally had meant when she had spoken about ants. It really felt quite like that. My head was full of ants running around inside my skull. If people were to know what it feels like when a Mentalist goes inside their brain, if they could ever remember, they would never say that it is a good thing that they even exist. Because it is quite simply an abominable sensation.

The ant feeling left abruptly, once he understood that he was not getting his desired result. I guess he tried to get into Lucas' and Ricky's head as well because I saw them both wince one after the other, but it didn't last long. Remaining silent, he turned toward Sally and scanned downwards until stopping and staring at her belly. She smiled and spoke to him gently. She said that she knew.

She also said that she was ready to stay but only if he erased our records and gave us our lives back. She meant us four, the men of our group. That had not been what we planned but I did not dare interrupt their exchange.

The Mentalist did not respond. He focused his strange eyes on us, as if to measure the weight of this demand. I do not really know how to explain it, but I'm sure he hesitated because several times he turned and gave me a lingering look. If Lucas had not waved his gun around at him, who knows? Maybe the scales would have tipped in our favor, after all...

But the threat only had one result. His face hardened, and he shook his head no. I then realized that our luck was gone and that I should have realized it from the start.

He was already too old, too experienced, neither emotional nor persuadable enough. His mission would soon end and he knew it. We had stumbled upon a Mentalist who would never cede anything to us. If he had been a few years younger, it might have been possible to shake him up enough to scare him a little or push him into doing something. But this one was far too old to want to help us.

Karl must have come to the same conclusion because his attitude suddenly changed. He got into the van, pushed me backwards towards Lucas and quietly pointed his gun at the Mentalist. Sally screamed "no!" but Karl's arm had not finished moving. The gun continued its movement and came to a stop in front of her belly, its barrel pressed against her navel.

I wanted to intervene, but Lucas grabbed me. Ricky was petrified. I could only see Karl from the back and the Mentalist's face remained expressionless, as if he were somewhere else. Sally's expression was gentle and calm. It was as if she had planned the situation and was not particularly surprised. She almost seemed relieved when she glanced over at me one last time.

The shot rang out inside the van and I thought my ears were going to explode. Behind me, Lucas and Ricky shot at each other simultaneously. The Mentalist had not lost time regaining control and had chosen those who were the most accessible to him. Karl did not leave him the time to take control of us and had put a bullet in his head before Sally had even finished collapsing onto the floor of the van. The scene had lasted only a few seconds.

In the middle of the pools of blood, four more bodies were thus added to our slate: a woman, two men and a twelve year old kid with strange eyes and the hair of an old man.

Barely more than two minutes to go now… that's all the time left for me to wrap things up. To think about Karl, who should have been standing here next to me today.

Two minutes before kicking the bucket and reaping my reward.

4 – THE CELL

THE CELL

Karl died three days ago. Three days before the date of our sentencing.

When the Center wardens picked us up on the road, alerted by the fact of the Mentalist's delay, I was lying on the pavement, in the same place where Sally had lain down. Karl was sitting on the stony beach and had given up trying to speak to me.

I had refused to leave with him, to give him the code, or even simply to talk with him. His threatening me with his gun had only made me laugh in his face. I told him to fuck off before lying down on the asphalt and closing my eyes. I was hoping he would shoot me or split somewhere and leave me alone, but it would seem that he didn't want to deprive himself of my company.

The guards thus arrested us and shipped us off to where you would expect us to go. Into a cell.

Time had never seemed to drag on for so long as when in Karl's company. We shared a three-by-four meter space for over a month. During all that time, I had the impression that the walls were moving in closer every day and that they would eventually suffocate me.

The first week, he tried the angle of "We need to stick together- just between us unlucky fellows". Exposing his personal secrets after lights out, his life story, his unhappy childhood... leaving nothing out, he seemed to enjoy his monologue. Karl loved listening to himself talk.

I lost track of how many times he tried to wheedle the account's access code out of me. But these attempts lacked any conviction by that time. It seemed that he only tried through habit or reflex, more to pass the time rather than to obtain any result.

Because I think he was perfectly aware that I would never tell him and that it was all to no avail.

The second week, when he got tired of chattering all alone and finally understood that I wasn't going to speak to him, he started trying to freak me out. So he described a whole lot of foul tales about the fate of those in our situation and made out the list of tortures set up for the killers of a Mentalist. A category of criminals so rare that the case had only appeared twice before us, according to him. Thus a very special treatment was reserved, the description of which was clearly intended to make me weep or throw up. But those stories didn't interest me any more than the ones about his life and I only wanted one thing: that he'd stop bothering me so I could sleep.

So, when the third week began, he decided to mess around with my sleep. Simulated snoring and groaning, tapping against the metal parts of the bed, scratching the wall, singing… He started pulling out all the stops to prevent me from getting a wink of sleep. I did not want to satisfy him by responding, but my face the next day was probably enough to make him understand that his tactic had worked. So obviously, he continued. What had only been a stupid pastime initially then became a sort of vicious mission for him: to drive me crazy.

At first, all that surprised me. His behavior did not correspond to the Karl I had known up until then. I wondered what game he was playing. At this stage of our stay in the cell, he should have been trying to become a model prisoner and keep in line. Instead, he seemed to regress and lose control.

I remembered his box of drug patches that he took with him everywhere and the knife he used to take out in times of stress to calm his nerves. I think that Karl found his withdrawal symptoms difficult to deal with and so his deep underlying inclinations were rising to the surface. The guy was psychologically twisted and this really began to show. For the first time, I saw his face exhibit expressions of panic, those of a man who sincerely believes that his life is in danger. In my opinion, he was just undergoing serious problems from needing a fix and I was the only thing he had on hand to focus his loathing on.

Among other substances, Karl must have used tons of anti-sleep patches during his lifetime, to have such little need for sleep. That is the only possible valid explanation that I could think of. Either that or the guy was not even human. Whatever the case, I couldn't manage to keep up with him. The lack of sleep first gave me horrendous migraines, then dizziness and problems seeing straight. When I managed to doze off and then the sounds he made woke me up with a start, I found that most of the time he was quietly asleep, wrapped up in his blankets. I started to wonder which sounds were real and which came from inside my head.

From time to time, it was a prolonged silence that woke me up, as if that were the anomaly. Sitting up on my bunk, I'd discover him seated in front of me, watching me with a strange little smile. When he was certain that I would not get back to sleep, he'd stretch out without a word and go back to snoring.

After a couple of weeks, I was shaking and had problems expressing myself without trying to find my words. My eyes burned and I'd never yawned so much in my life. I felt weighed down, slow and lost.

The problem was the isolation in which we were sadistically kept together. It wasn't the few contacts in the visiting room from time to time that could change the impression that my world was reduced to Karl alone.

Karl and his strange eyes that followed me everywhere. Karl and his precise movements, overly calm for a guy in his situation, even though his hands would sometimes shake. Karl and his little smile that made me want to scream until someone could come and do me the favor of knocking me out. But nobody ever came, other than to deliver meals.

I ended up thinking my true condemnation was to stay with him for all eternity. I stopped counting the days, and I realized that perhaps it was expected of us to work things out between ourselves. To do ourselves what was required, so that only one of us remained. Karl must have come to the same conclusion by then, because he went into overdrive with his madness, which he brought up to an even higher level.

I caught him spitting in my plate and pissing in my water. He made fun of me when I lost control and I sent my tray flying against the wall screaming for a warden to intervene. Of course, nobody showed up.

I started keeping track of when the food was brought to us as if I were starving, just to be sure that he wouldn't do it again. So he just changed his tactics back to his little night games. This time though, he also went after my few clothes, tearing up what he could with his teeth. Upon awakening, I only had the clothes still on my back, other than the rags he had made and that he had also thrown into the toilet just to finish off the job.

Oddly, it was at this point that I started to think that he might really end up by killing me. When he invaded my personal space and started destroying my few possessions. I really didn't have much. Once he had finished with my two books, my comb and my toothpaste, he would surely go after me. What else could he do?

Three days ago, we were taken to the showers, for one of our bi-weekly scrubbing sessions. Even there, we were always left alone. I would have given anything to share the session with a group of ten strangers rather than with Karl. But our isolation was permanent, if you don't count the fact that the Module has its eyes everywhere.

While I was soaping up and trying to ignore him, he came over whistling an old nursery rhyme. For the first time I really noticed his gnarled arms, narrow chest and the incredible amount of body hair growing all over him. He looked too white, too bony and too animal-like. I am unable to explain why, but seeing him up close this way suddenly made me nauseous.

When he suddenly stopped singing, he then told me with a big smile that just after firing he could make out a bit of the baby that had been inside Sally's body. I vomited.

Down on my knees on the cracked shower tiles, I threw up my most recent meal, while he continued to describe in detail something that I had tried to suppress in my head for weeks. A baby transformed into mush inside the womb. A future Mentalist who could never bother anyone. A great service for humanity. An action for which he was proud, and had almost made him come… He dumped a whole list of nasty ideas on me without stopping until I stood up and grabbed him around the throat.

Apparently I didn't squeeze tight enough because he laughed before singing out that between those who were engendering Mentalists and those who were sterile, the world was going up shit's creek.

He added that fortunately there were still normal and virile guys like him. Like him, but not like me.

In saying that, he stared at my balls with an amused look and then began laughing like a lunatic. As if it was the best joke in the world and as if I wasn't holding onto his throat with my hands. In fact, he never struggled.

I started to shake him back and forth, to make him shut up. But his laughter never ceased. The more I moved my arms the more he just made fun of me with a bug-eyed look which ended up making me as crazy as he.

The lack of sleep, my bunched up nerves and the fear that he was trying to do me in, were all jumbled up inside me. But I'd be lying if I said that all this made me start squeezing harder. The truth is that I just wanted him to stop laughing. The sound coming out of his mouth had simply become unbearable and pushed me over the edge.

Karl died three days ago because I smashed his skull against the shower stall walls, hitting him against them as many times as was needed to silence him. When I finally let go of his neck, I was covered with a mixture of dried soap, vomit and blood.

I sat in a corner and then it was my turn to laugh like crazy until they finally came to get me. They hosed me down with cold water to rinse me off, but more especially to calm me down. I laughed because I came to understand that Karl, although he had become half crazy, was more clever than I had been.

Three days before the Judgment day, I killed a man for the first time in my life. What an idiot I was to crack up so close to the end. An idiot not to understand that what he wanted was simply to take me down along with him.

Behind me, I can finally hear him moving around. There is only a little more than a minute remaining before I have to answer the last question. The Guardian moves over from my right and stands in front of me. He is calm, attentive and almost respectful. He looks at his watch and then crosses his arms. Oddly, the only thing that annoys me is that he can lower his eyes and see the hole in my sock.

But he is polite right to the end and looks at me straight in the face.

"Jeremy, it's time. You now need to let me know your decision. Do you choose to submit to the Judgment or would you rather give up?"

I have thirty seconds or so to answer him and I have absolutely no fucking idea what I'm going to say. The Guardian will perhaps be polite up to the last minute, but I am simply pitiful. Right up to the end.

5 – THE ROPE

The first time I met the Guardian was in the visiting room of the Center. I had been told I had a visitor and I still vaguely hoped of seeing my ex-wife, even though that seemed highly unlikely.

The day she had discovered that I was one of the sterile population, which I had been hiding from her for four years, she had thrown me out and told me to never speak to her again without her lawyer present. The fact that I was sentenced to twenty years for grand larceny, before our divorce was even finalized, had not made her any more affectionate, might be the least one could say.

Anyway, entering the visiting room that day, I was hoping, though without much conviction, that it would be her. But it was not my ex-wife waiting for me there, nor the skinny guy with glasses who came from time to time to speak to me about my appeal. It had been weeks since he had shown any sign of life. He must have gotten fed up with traveling here for nothing.

My visitor was a guy I had never seen before. A former Mentalist, based on the color of his eyes. I have always been suspicious of those we call the Reclassified. They've lost the gift but they still have a kind of charisma which is more powerful than average. They can easily bamboozle you if you're not careful.

So I was suspicious but my curiosity was stronger than my desire to do an about-face. I should probably have listened to my initial gut feeling, when I look back at things now. Because in under an hour the rest of my life was to be determined in that visitor's room. I remember the conversation quite well, which started out in the most banal way.

"Thank you for agreeing to meet me, Jeremy."

"I take advantage of any distractions I can when they come up. It was either that or my fourth nap of the day. So you are…?" I asked.

"I am the Guardian," he said.

During this initial exchange, I was slouching uncomfortably on the metal chair. His serious tone of voice made me sit up, the idea being to look a bit more presentable.

"The Guardian? Meaning…? Guardian of what?"

"Of the Trapdoor," he said.

"You're not helping me much here. A trapdoor where? Why do you guard it?" I asked.

The man looked amused.

"I forgot that you do not get to follow what is happening on the outside. It is surprising to meet someone who is not yet aware of things," he stated.

"Sorry to disappoint you, but time is somewhat at… a standstill in this place. You will need to bring me up to date and explain why you are visiting me," I suggested.

"I wanted to meet you because you are on my list."

He put up his hand when I started to open my mouth to ask him, obviously, what list he was referring to.

"Let me first tell you about the reasons for my coming here and then I will answer all of your questions, ok?" he asked.

I didn't really have any choice, so I nodded while grumbling in vague agreement.

"You were given a twenty-year irreducible sentence, if my notes are accurate. Multiple theft of vehicles along with hacking into security systems. A sentence which you probably think is quite severe."

So I quipped: "Well, we all know the penalty scale… I knew

what to expect when I did things. But you must understand that the temptation can be pretty high, when you know that you will never have any other means required to obtain an Autonomous Travel Authorization" – which would have enabled me to have my own car and travel legally.

"The people I stole cars from were able to buy another one the next day. I was tired of walking," I continued.

"The rules were established for valid reasons, Jeremy. The optimization of energy resources, to control pollution thresholds…"

"Don't try to make me cry. The latest generation of vehicles pollute less than a dog pissing on a sidewalk. Speak rather of controlling people circulating and their freedom. You know as well as I do that the sterile, the old and the inactive, never have priority. For that and for everything else. We are second-class citizens," I threw back.

"But it is thanks to all of our rules that we were able to make so much collective progress. Indeed, I recognize that some difficulties should be taken into account and I understand your dissatisfaction," he said.

I could not help laughing because the guy really seemed to believe what he was saying.

"You are priceless. Here you are jerking me around, which I should find annoying, instead strangely enough I kind of like you. Are you messing with my brain?" I asked.

"I'm too old for that, as you know. I became Reclassified ages ago."

"So, at this point you guard a trapdoor? That's an interesting change of direction."

"*The* Trapdoor. If you had not been locked up, you would

know what it is. Before talking to you about it, I would just like to know… If you could get out of here today, what would you do with your life?"

I had pondered that very question before and still not found an answer. After all, I had another nineteen years ahead of me to find one.

"Let's see… find a woman, who is sterile too, and who enjoys my company. Buy a nice house somewhere, lost in the middle of nowhere. Die peacefully asleep in my bed when I'm very old. Except no, that's not possible. Those of us who are sterile have a lower life expectancy. That's one of those "difficulties" you were mentioning," I quipped.

"You are thirty-four, right?" he asked.

"Your notes are up to date, yes."

"When you get out, you will have about a decade or so left to enjoy your freedom," he stated.

"Pretty much. If I am one of the lucky ones. Ten years to wonder about the meaning of life. That may become a bit monotonous…" I joked.

"At least you've kept your sense of humor."

"I'm not sure I'll still have it by the time they let me out. Just between you and me, don't you find all this a bit ironic?"

He looked at me with an expression of surprise and curiosity. I said to myself that I quite liked this guy. He was not completely narrow-minded.

"In what way?" he asked.

"You Mentalists are demigods at birth and live your life backwards, needing to transform later on by regressing to becoming nearly unknown. Whereas we, being among those who are sterile, spend our lives trying to lift ourselves up before it's too late, starting from the lowest rung of the ladder. Our paths go in opposite directions, but we all have the same enemy: time."

"I'd never seen things from that angle. It's interesting," he responded.

"It's especially a load of nonsense. Do you really think that's how things were planned by our ancestors? A world with sterile people, Mentalists and ten per cent of the population locked up in these Centers? Perhaps our history books don't tell us everything, but I'm not sure this is what they had in mind when they created the world government one hundred and fifty years ago," I said.

"You forget the benefits. The end of all wars, a higher standard of living on a global scale, a more equitable distribution of opportunity and access to resources for populations everywhere. In the last century, entire continents were plagued with poverty."

"Today, poverty exists only in the minds of those required to pay the price."

"I think you are exaggerating because you are on the wrong side of the barrier. I understand that your stay in the Center must make you feel a little bitter. But I admit that there is a major problem," he said.

He leaned toward me, crossing his arms on the table. His voice dropped to say something secretive.

"The population is bored to death."

"I beg your pardon?"

"By wanting to overly clean up or correct the mistakes of the past, the founders of the global system eradicated certain things which are really essential. Creativity and flights of fantasy, along with the unexpected, are some of these. The Module over-controls way too much so people never have the impression they will be surprised or even feel alive. Everything they do, what they eat, their hobbies, who they meet… everything runs so well; life has become insipid," he said.

"Insipid? I would not have chosen that word."

"But you understand what I mean… this total lack of passion, of excitement. Unfortunately, interventions by the High Mentalist are no longer enough to keep the population happy. It is as if their effect has lost some of its intensity every time it's been used. The government is now aware of the situation," he stated.

"I congratulate them on their analysis and I'm sorry that your six-year old former boss has had trouble doing his job well. But what does all this have to do with me? You mentioned a list…"

"I'm coming to that. In short, we believe that by allowing people to live vicariously through the lives of some criminals, this might add a bit of spice to their lives. Obviously by reminding them at the same time that leading an honest life is preferable."

I had been prepared to hear about a whole lot of things, but not this. My expression must have been amusing because the man smiled.

"The Trapdoor is a program, Jeremy. In three months, we are launching a show to be broadcast by the Module throughout the entire planet, which we expect will enthrall the public. Just enough to satisfy cravings of pent-up violence which clutters up rather too many minds."

"A program? You're saying a thing like where you would invite prisoners to repent in public?" I asked.

"No, that would be of no interest to most people. Not for long, in any case. I'm talking about an adventure game show in its full splendor. A program that would allow people to experience an entire criminal event almost live, while it occurs. And I'm here to offer you the opportunity to become a participant, because you are here on my list."

He took out a sheet of paper which outlined what he offered. He handed the paper over to me and continued commenting from memory. Suddenly, his mentalist robot-like reflexes appeared to come back to him.

"Eight participants, selected with care from among the prison's population of the Centers, for a game that will last for three months. We select candidates from among all types of criminals, with the exception of rapists, serial killers and all those having been found guilty of a premeditated violent crime. They would generally be considered too unmanageable. The rule is simple: by participating, your current sentence is canceled… if you go all the way to the end of the game," he recited.

"And by end, you mean…?"

"The Judgment at the Trapdoor. Applied to all those who are still participating on the final day."

While my mouth dropped open a bit wider, making me look even more like an idiot, he continued to reveal the other rules involved.

"Among other things, you are required to accomplish a successful holdup. This motivates both the participants and the public… it adds a little fantasy and spices up the game, you see."

"Uh, yeah. I mean, I suppose," I stammered.

"I should say that the Warton-Schaff Bank has been kind enough to sponsor the show and obviously agreed to lose a few million urkans. If the hold-up is not satisfactorily performed within the time limit, the game stops. In addition the participant or participants who are still around for the Judgment must be in possession of this money if they are to be freed. I need to indicate that if anyone thinks they can simply escape they are monitored by an electronic bracelet. The producers know where you are at all times even if they will only request the Module to intervene if necessary. The participants must have the possibility of being successful of course. These bracelets are also equipped with micro-cameras which record everything you do. It will be by editing these images for broadcast, as well as using images from the Module which has also reserved a specific channel for our use, that we will be able to put together some interesting programs on a daily basis."

"But if people can see what is going on, then the participants won't have a chance! All the cops in the area will be on their tail within two minutes!" I blurted out.

"There will be a one-day delay in broadcast. Enough for you to always have a little head-start. That way, with a bit of planning and common sense, a clever mind can make all the difference. It will be up to the group being organized and for each member to develop their own strategy that will take them as far as possible. You will have weapons, safe-houses and access to various useful bits of information," he stated.

"I understand."

In truth, I didn't really understand a thing. The situation seemed absurd to me, and I was totally lost. Then I asked lots of questions and the Guardian patiently brought me up to speed. Obviously, at the end of our interview, I accepted his proposal. As I already said, the idea seemed like a good one at the time. In hindsight, I think maybe I should have done my remaining nineteen years…

Our second meeting was held on the launch day of the program. The Guardian introduced everyone, reviewed the rules, provided our equipment and made a magnificent speech which would certainly be used as an introduction to the first program to be broadcast the following day. Most of the other participants looked as lost as I did and if I could still have withdrawn at that point, I think I would have. But Lana's eyes and Sally's belly took away any desire I might have to take off like a bat out of hell. The well-known nice-guy part of me that was already acting up.

The Guardian reappeared at regular intervals while I was waiting with Karl until the Judgment Day in our cell. The cell was located in this reconstituted Center that had been set up for the show. He lent a sympathetic ear to my complaints and upon leaving the visitor's room, which acted as the daily confessional setting for the program, asked me to try to be patient. But four days ago, for the first time, he allowed himself to give me some advice.

"Be very careful, Jeremy, you're running out of time. And don't forget that only one participant will be released."

Was it this phrase which followed me into the shower? I don't really know. What is certain is that Karl was convinced he'd have no chance of getting a favorable Judgment, even though nobody can say how right or wrong he was. After all, who knows if killing a Mentalist might not actually add points rather than take them away? Maybe you can even become a hero that way… But it did seem unlikely to me and Karl must have shared my opinion.

He also knew that I would leave as a rich man, if I were the one to be given a second chance. I think that was the idea that he couldn't accept, more than anything else. Karl was not the kind to let himself sink without trying to bring you under with him. And my drowning is taking much longer than his. One hour with a rope around your neck is not really my idea of fun.

The Guardian looks me in the eyes and repeats his question. The sixty minutes of deliberation will soon be over and the Judgment will be announced. I only have a few seconds remaining before I am required to respond, if I want to leave the game and return to my nineteen-year sentence. If I don't say anything… the rules are quite clear. By remaining silent, one consents.

I try one last time to figure out my chances. Will Karl's murder be pardoned? He was a real piece of scum, after all. I have sort of avenged Sally, in a way. But as I am the last one and I'm still here, that may be because I am really the worst one of them all. In that case, they will probably condemn me.

The Judgment, or giving up? A probable death on one hand or else all those empty years in a cell. A few years ago, I was tired of walking. Today, I am tired of waiting and putting up with everything.

"I choose to submit myself to the Judgment."

The second hand finishes going around just afterwards. For once in my life, I'm not late.

The Guardian thanks me for answering and heads toward the curtain that hides the wall in front of me, just under the clock and the camera which has been immortalizing the entire scene.

In the old days, prisoners sentenced to death were subjected to being watched by the families of their victims. Here there is no mirror showing me trembling as I stand on the trapdoor. Only two digital screens displaying the numbers that will trigger its opening… or not. The Guardian carefully re-explained the expected protocol during his last visit to the visitor's room. He is quite a precise and organized man.

On the left side, the votes in favor of my freedom. On the right, those who want the rope. The largest number will prevail. If I had not killed Karl, the choice would have been between him and me. By killing him, I was condemned to compete against myself.

More than two billion viewers are connected to the Module around the world. Most of them must have voted, that's for sure. It is so rare to be asked their opinion about anything whatsoever. The Guardian told me it had been years since there had been such a popular event and that the entire planet was talking about me.

I don't want to look at the screens and so I focus on the hole in my sock in order not to glance toward the wall. Only one question haunts me.

Could I have played any better?

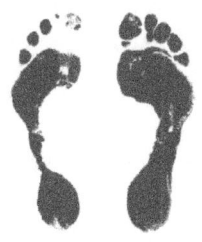

Acknowledgments

We would like to once again thank all of our "beta-readers" for their perusal, their advice, their suggestions and their constructive criticism.

Special thanks to Kristen and Ceilidh, Philippe, Hervé, Celine, Pascal and Guy, who had already participated in the "Remoras" adventure and yet still helped out this time as well.

If you liked "The Trapdoor", if you want to share this adventure with other readers or you want to provide us with your opinion, do not forget to leave a note on our Amazon feedback page.

Thank you!

M.I.A and John H. Temple

The authors

Nom de plume M.I.A (Missing In Action) embodies the meeting of two friends (Hélène and Sébastien) both passionate about literature, cinema and political news, to mention only a few obvious things we have in common.

Our working method is particular because more than 1 500 kilometers separate us: who would think that our books were fully worked out and written by communicating remotely?

Go to leblogmia.com to learn more!

By the same authors

Did you like this short story? If you haven't read it yet, we recommend that you read "Remoras", our novel first released in December 2012 (English version), which lays the foundations of the universe you have just discovered and to which "The Trapdoor" makes a few references to…

The original French version of this novel – "Rémoras", released in February 2012 and also available on Amazon – stayed in the French Kindle Top 100 for more than 220 days. The book was also optioned for TV adaptation in the US, in June 2013.

Here is the summary:

"Only puny secrets need protection. Big discoveries are protected by public incredulity". Marshall McLuhan

Following eight years of retirement, a trio of French intelligence agents must again take up arms to defend against a "cleansing" operation initiated by their former employers. Their response launches a series of global cataclysms, transforming the world for all time.

What is the true nature of these reformed black ops agents? Who are they? Will they prevail in this contest with "The Circle", a mysterious clandestine organization that seems to control every aspect of the society world-wide?

"Remoras" weaves aspects of political fiction and the thriller, while skillfully delivering a master-crafted story inspired by true events in the everyday news.

Explore where truth breaks free from fact.

Illustrated edition also available

The 518 page printed version of the novel is laid out in 60 chapters and divided into the following:

Prologue

Part 1: Opening Moves

Part 2: Development

Part 3: The "Priapus" Attack

Part 4: The "Carpet" Attack

Part 5: The "Vulcan" Attack

Part 6: Check

Part 7: Zugzwang

Part 8: Mate

Epilogue

Retrouvez tous les titres et l'actualité des Éditions HJ :

Sur notre site Internet :

http://www.editionshelenejacob.com

Sur Facebook :

https://www.facebook.com/EditionsHJ

Sur Twitter :

https://twitter.com/EditionsHJ